Kimmi and the Sea Dragon

The Mermaids of
Crystal Cay

Kimmi and the
Sea Dragon

J. B. Moonstar

Published By: The Little Horsemen an imprint of 4 Horsemen Publications, Inc.

The Little Horsemen Publications
℅ 4 Horsemen Publications, Inc.
PO Box 419
Sylva, NC 28779
4horsemenpublications.com
info@4horsemenpublications.com

Cover by J. Kotick
Typesetting by Niki Tantillo
Edited by CI Stearns

Library of Congress Control Number: 2022951911

Paperback ISBN-13: 978-1-64450-806-0
Hardcover ISBN-13: 978-1-64450-807-7
Audiobook ISBN-13: 978-1-64450-809-1
Ebook ISBN-13: 978-1-64450-808-4

Dedication

This book is dedicated to Diana Renn and Creature Conserve, for their valuable assistance and support as I searched for the information and resources to create a mermaid world for the Mermaids of Crystal Cay. Thank you for your guidance, as well as for your continuous work in bringing artists and scientists together in a joint effort to protect and save endangered species!

Dear Reader,

Welcome to my world!

During a recent hurricane, I was able to help a local mermaid find a young manatee who was trapped by the storm. To avoid the high winds and choppy waters during the rescue, I was given a magic amulet that would allow me to become a mermaid and swim under water!

After young Ethan was safe, Alleana, the leader of the Crystal Cay mermaids, asked me if I wanted to become part of her pod. She told me if I kept it a secret from other humans, I could use the magic amulet to visit them whenever I wanted, and she would reach out to me if she needed my help again.

There are so many stories to tell about the mermaids of Crystal Cay! Please join me on the first adventure of a mermaid named Kimmi who has been chosen to raise a young sea dragon until it is large enough to live with its parents in the open ocean. Although warned not to go beyond the reef with her charge, when Kimmi's necklace breaks and her pearls scatter into open water, they forget the warning and swim out to find the lost pearls.

What will they find? What will find them? And will they make it back to the safety of the reef? Join Kimmi and Snappy on their adventures beyond the reef—because where these two go, adventure follows!

Wishing you a magical day!

Michelle
Part-time mermaid

Table of Contents

Chapter One

Arrival of the Sea Dragons

"Kimmi, where are you?" Alleana shouted through the cave. The leader of the Crystal Cay mermaid pod was getting worried that a required attendee was still not in attendance.

"I'll be right there!" Kimmi called back, swimming quickly through the connecting tunnel to get to Alleana's cave, her long ruby-red hair tangled with several seashells that she tried to straighten with her fingers as she entered the cave. "Here I am!"

"Where have you been? You know the sea dragons will be here any moment now, we need to be ready!" Alleana replied once Kimmi was back in her cave.

"I know, I can't wait to play with a real sea dragon!" Kimmi replied excitedly.

"You are not to just play with him, Kimmi, you need to raise him and protect him until he is big enough to live out in the ocean with his family, do you understand?" Alleana scolded her, hoping for once that Kimmi was listening to her. "And don't take him beyond the reef!"

"Of course, Alleana," Kimmi said, trying to sound serious. "I will take very good care of him! Don't worry, we will stay close to home. How hard can it be to take care of a baby sea dragon?"

"You'll soon find out how hard it can be! Now untangle your hair, straighten your necklace, and go to the front chamber and wait for their arrival!" Alleana said, shaking her head, not sure if Kimmi knew what she had gotten herself into.

Alleana's pod had been asked to care for the young son of a family of sea dragons living off the coast. This was not an unusual request, as even though adult sea dragons are enormous, their children start off as tiny sea dragons and are too small to be safe in the big ocean. Since it became too dangerous for adult sea dragons to remain in shallow waters while their young grow into their sea dragon scales, the mermaids have taken over raising them from shortly after they are born until they are big enough to swim with their parents in the deep water.

Alleana's experience taught her that baby sea dragons also needed to be taught how to interact with other sea creatures while living with the mermaid pod, so that once they are big, they were able to watch out for smaller residents—big sea dragons have big responsibilities!

Roselia, the normal sea dragon nanny, was not available, so Kimmi gladly volunteered to watch the new sea dragon, but she had never even seen one before. The past few days had been spent teaching Kimmi what was needed to properly raise a young sea dragon; however, Alleana was not too sure how much Kimmi would remember.

Keeping Kimmi still to teach her all she needed to know on how to raise a baby sea dragon was difficult. Swimming in circles or chasing a stray fish that wandered into the cave, Kimmi was too excited to stay still and listen to Alleana's instructions!

As Alleana joined Kimmi in the main chamber, she watched Kimmi swimming around the entrance. She called out, "Kimmi, come stay by me so they have enough room to enter, okay?" The main chamber was lit from an opening in the ceiling, with the sun filtering down through the water, giving them light. It was large enough to accommodate adult sea dragons, but it would be tight.

"Yes, Alleana!" Kimmi replied as she quickly swam back and positioned herself next to Alleana.

"Now, remember what I've taught you," Alleana reminded her yet again. "You are his protector and teacher, not just a playmate, okay?"

"Yes, I will remember!" Kimmi said absent-mindedly; her eyes wide and focused on the cave entrance, waiting to see her first sea dragon.

Suddenly, a loud roar echoed through the chamber, announcing the arrival of the sea dragon family.

"They're here!" Alleana whispered to Kimmi. "Remember, bow to the mom and dad, and follow my lead!" Alleana swam out toward the middle of the chamber with Kimmi following behind. With just her and Kimmi inside, the cave looked huge; however, Alleana knew that once the sea dragons entered, it would feel a bit crowded.

"Please enter, Ferdinand and Alexis, you are welcome!" Alleana called out loudly.

The sea dragons entered the cave one at a time, they were too large to enter together. As Kimmi watched in amazement, she got her first glimpse of these magnificent ocean creatures. Long, slender, and covered with shiny scales, they were beautiful! Moving smoothly and coiling their tails once inside the cave, they bowed to Alleana, and Alleana bowed back. After Alleana reached back and tapped Kimmi on the shoulder, Kimmi bowed too.

"Greetings, Ferdinand and Alexis," Alleana called out to them. "Welcome to my cave, we are glad to have you here. It is our honor to have Fernando Manuel visit with us. Thank you!"

"Greetings, Alleana," Alexis called out to her. "Thank you for having Fernando as your guest. We greatly appreciate you and your pod watching over him during these first few months."

Something small popped out from between Alexis and Ferdinand, swimming slowly toward Alleana. It was a tiny creature, maybe only a foot long, in stark contrast to the giant size of Alexis and Ferdinand, who were a least thirty feet in length. Leafy appendages were sticking out all over its body, waving back and forth as little by little it made its way toward the mermaids.

Unable to wait any longer, Kimmi started swimming swiftly toward the little creature—she had to see what it looked like!

"Kimmi," Alleana called anxiously. "Stay back; you should wait for permission!"

But Kimmi didn't heed the warning, she was too excited. As she got closer, the tiny creature stretched out its neck and snapped at Kimmi's hand. Pulling her hand back in time to avoid being bitten, she turned and swam quickly back to Alleana and hid behind her, not sure she wanted to meet this little thing anymore.

Alexis called out sharply, "Snappy, stop that!"

The little creature looked back at his mom with sad eyes and pouted; then he turned around and started slowly swimming back to her, his little leafy appendages swaying back and forth like seaweed as he swam.

Ferdinand explained apologetically to Alleana and Kimmi, "We are sorry. Fernando just got his baby teeth and is learning how to bite, so he tries to bite everything he sees. We have taken to calling him Snappy."

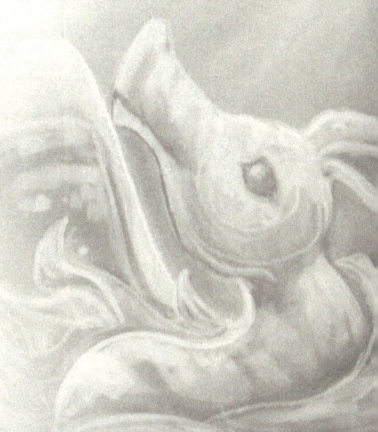

Chapter Two

FORMAL INTRODUCTIONS

Alleana swam out gracefully to the small dragon, stopping about ten feet away and smiled at him, calling out, "So nice to meet you, Snappy!"

But Kimmi stayed behind, she didn't want to get any closer. As Alleana waved for Kimmi to come toward her, Alleana said to Snappy, "Snappy, I want you to meet Kimmi! She is going to take care of you for a few months until you get a little bigger and can go live with your parents in the big ocean. I'm sure you will have lots of fun together!"

Snappy started slowly swimming toward the mermaids again, looking like a floating ball of seaweed. Kimmi hesitantly swam to where Alleana was waiting, stopping behind her and peeking around Alleana's shoulder. Looking a little fearfully at Snappy, afraid he might snap at her again, she said softly, "Nice to meet you, Snappy. How are you today?"

"Hi, Kimmi! My mom said we would have lots of fun playing in the caves!" Snappy said happily. "What do you want to do first?"

As Kimmi looked back at the baby sea dragon, not sure what to say, Snappy's mom leaned her head closer to the mermaids.

"Hi, Kimmi," Alexis said in a friendly manner. "It is so nice to meet you, and I thank you for agreeing to watch over Fernando for a few months. He is a nice dragon; he just doesn't know how to react to others yet. He's never even seen a mermaid before. I'm sorry that he snapped at you—he has been doing that a lot lately!"

"Oh, okay," replied Kimmi, still a little shy. "I'm sure we can work it out."

"Well, Fernando," Ferdinand said to his son. "If you are good here, your mother and I will leave you with these nice mermaids now. We will plan on picking you up once you have grown out of your camouflage leaves and have shiny scales like your mother and me!"

"I know you will have a lot of fun here; your sisters and brothers did! We are excited to see what color your scales will be! Take care, little Snappy, we will see you soon!" Ferdinand smiled and leaned down to rub snouts with his young son, and then turned and headed out of the cave, his shiny green scales sparkling in the water as he left.

"Bye, Dad," Snappy called out. "I'll see you again soon!"

Alexis leaned down to say goodbye to Snappy. "Snappy, my boy, you be nice to these mermaids, no snapping, okay?" she started with a little warning. "Make sure you listen to them, because they will teach you everything you need to know to be a big sea dragon like your father and me!" Her voice became softer and gentle as she continued. "Remember, Fernando, your father and I will miss you and look forward to you joining us once you get a little bigger.

Make sure you do what the mermaids say, and we will be back before you know it!"

"Goodbye, Mom," Snappy replied, smiling at his mom. "I promise I'll be good! Thanks for letting me visit the mermaids!"

Leaning in, Alexis rubbed her son's snout with hers, and then turned to Alleana and Kimmi. "Thank you for watching over Fernando," she said appreciatively. "We are grateful for your help. If there are any problems, please do not hesitate to let me know. We will be back as soon as you send your signal!"

"Alleana," Alexis whispered softly with concern as she moved closer to her. "There is more activity past the reef, please make sure your pod and our little Fernando stay away from the area. Take care!" Then she turned and headed out of the cave, her purple scales shimmering in the water.

As Snappy watched his mom swim out the entrance, he went closer to Kimmi and looked up at her; now it was his turn to be a little shy. He looked at her with wide eyes and said softly, "I'm sorry for snapping at you, Kimmi, I promise I won't do it again, okay?"

A smile appeared on Kimmi's face as she looked at this tiny face with big eyes peeking out of his baby camouflage, and she replied happily, "Oh, Snappy, no worries, I'm sure we are going to have lots of fun together!"

Snappy's face lit up and a big smile appeared. "Thank you, Kimmi, I look forward to having fun. What's first?"

"Well," Kimmi said, then paused, thinking back to remember what Alleana had taught her. "Well, I think the first thing would be to figure out where you are going to sleep. I've made some room in my cave, let's go see if it works for you!" Kimmi turned and started swimming quickly toward her cave.

"Okay!" Snappy replied and started following her, but within seconds Kimmi was gone from sight down the tunnel. Snappy couldn't swim very fast, and when she disappeared, he stopped swimming and looked around fearfully, wondering what he should do next.

"Hey, Snappy," Alleana said softly as she swam up next to him. "Why don't I swim with you, and we'll go to Kimmi's cave together. She's never seen a baby sea dragon either, so you to will have to work together to become a great team, okay?"

"Thank you, Alleana!" Snappy replied as he looked toward the tunnel where Kimmi disappeared. "I'm sure we'll be able to work it out!"

Chapter Three

SOMEWHERE TO SLEEP

Reaching her sleeping cave, Kimmi spun around. She was excited to show Snappy where he would be sleeping, but he wasn't there! *Where is he?* Heading quickly back through the tunnel, she swam into Snappy and Alleana, slowly swimming her way.

"Hi, Kimmi," Alleana said softly. "Baby dragons can't swim as fast as mermaids, remember?"

"Oh, yeah ... I'm sorry I swam away, Snappy," Kimmi said apologetically as she swam over to him. "I promise I won't leave you again. Please forgive me!"

"It's okay, Kimmi," Snappy responded with a smile. "I know we have a lot to learn about each other before we are a team!"

"Thank you, Snappy, I promise I'll do my best to take care of you!" Kimmi smiled back, and the excitement returned to her voice as she continued. "I'm so thrilled to have you stay with us and couldn't wait to show you the nice place you will be sleeping!"

"Let's all swim together for a little bit, okay?" Alleana suggested. "Then you can see the right speed to swim with Snappy!"

"That's a good idea!" Kimmi said, swimming over next to Snappy. "I'm so excited you are here; we are going to have so much fun!"

The trio headed down the tunnel, and as the light faded Kimmi swam closer to Snappy. "Are you okay, Snappy?" she asked. "It is only a little farther until we get to my sleeping cave."

"I'm okay, Kimmi," he replied. "Thanks for swimming slowly so I can keep up with you!"

The tunnel grew lighter as they got closer to Kimmi's cave, as the skylights allowed the sun to shine through. "Here we are!" Kimmi called out as she swam ahead and went over to a large rock that was covered in soft sand. "Here is where I sleep!" she said as she pointed to the sandy pile.

Once Snappy got to the cave, she swam over to him and led him slowly in the direction of a large pot against the wall of the cave. In the pot were various types of seaweed, most several feet tall. There were leaves of various colors—red, green, blue, brown, even orange—all swaying gently with the current flowing through the cave.

"Look, Snappy," she called to him excitedly as they swam toward the pot, pointing to a section of seaweed. "What do you think? You can rest here on the leaves. Alleana made sure there were stems so you could wrap your tail around them, so you don't drift off." Kimmi stopped next to the seaweed and let Snappy swim closer.

"I hope you like it!" she exclaimed. "I worked hard to get it like they told me!"

"This is nice, and I do like it," Snappy answered cheerfully as he slowly approached. "I think I should be very comfortable here."

Snappy swam through the first layer of seaweed and disappeared as his camouflage blended in with the leaves.

"Where did you go?" Kimmi asked, looking into the seaweed. As she swam around the pot trying to see where he was hiding, she called out, "How did you do that?"

"That's my camouflage!" Snappy replied happily. "It helps me blend into the seaweed, so you have to look very close to find me!" At that point he popped his face out of a stand of seaweed, his big eyes beaming. "This is going to be fun!"

"Alright, you two," Alleana called. "I'll let you play hide and seek for a few minutes, and then you will have to start your chores. Everyone must do their fair share!" As she headed toward the entrance to the cave, she added, "Remember, Kimmi, you have to keep Snappy with you at all times, no swimming off, okay?"

"Okay, Alleana, I won't swim off without him," Kimmi answered back, turning to watch her as she left the cave. Snappy took that moment to pull his head back into the seaweed and was hidden again.

"Where did you go? I'm going to find you!" She called to him, smiling and giggling, as they started a game of hide and seek. Snappy continued swimming between the seaweed and hiding, and Kimmi tried to spot him. Each time she found him she called out, "There you are!" and pointed at him. Then he would hide once again under a different leaf. This lasted for several minutes, both enjoying their play time together.

"You know, Snappy," Kimmi said. "We will have to figure out how fast you can swim, so I don't leave you behind again. Is there a way to help you so you don't get left behind?"

"Well, sometimes my dad lets me ride on his back," Snappy answered. "But that doesn't work too well because the current knocks me off. He is so big the current doesn't bother him."

"But you are much littler, right? I understand!" Kimmi said with enthusiasm. "I know I can figure something out!" Swimming around her cave, she looked at various objects that she had found in the ocean and used as decorations. She wasn't sure what they were used for by whomever made them, but to her they were exciting, a window into another world. Her hair moved with the current, sometimes getting into her face as she was looking around.

"Hey, what if I put you in my hair?" she asked. "You could hold on with your tail, and you wouldn't get pulled off by my swimming or by the current."

Snappy's eyes widened as he looked at his leafy append-ages and then at her hair moving with the current all around her; he was not comfortable with this idea. "Well, um ... my camouflage may get tangled in your hair." He said timidly. "We may get so tangled together that you would have to cut your hair. That might not be a good idea. Any other ideas?"

Kimmi didn't like the idea of cutting her hair! She looked slowly at all the objects in her cave, what would work?

Chapter Four

HARVEST FOR DINNER

"I got it!" She called out as she swam over to the far corner of the cave and picked up a round object that was as large as Snappy. She turned it over and several small shells fell out, then she turned it upright again and held it by the wire handle.

"What do you think of this?" she asked as she quickly swam over to Snappy, holding the object in front of her. "I found this on one of my explores. It looks like you are to carry things in it, right? If you fit in it, I could carry you, and we would be together!"

Kimmi held up the object for Snappy to see. It was a large black object shaped like a sphere with the top cut off. There was a wire making an arch over the top that was attached on each side and formed a handle.

"It looks like you could fit inside, right? Is there enough room?" Kimmi asked anxiously, looking at the container and then at Snappy. She really wanted this to work, she liked to swim fast on her explores!

Swimming toward Snappy, she continued. "Alleana told me there are creatures who lose objects in the oceans, and that they may have used this to transport their items. She called it a kettle." Holding it by the handle in front of her, she practiced how she would swim if Snappy were inside, swishing her tail up and down while carefully making sure it stayed level.

"If you were inside, I wouldn't turn it over so you wouldn't fall out." She added to reassure him.

"Slow down for a moment," Snappy answered softly. "Let me see if I fit first, and then we can determine how you should hold it." At this point, he was not sure if this idea was going to work either.

Swimming slowly over to the kettle, he wiggled his body until he was mostly inside, only the top of his head was sticking out. "This could work!" he said with more enthusiasm. "What else do we need to worry about?"

"Well," Kimmi began. "If I lean over to pick something up, you may fall out. But we can make sure I don't turn it over, right? This is great! Let's practice!"

Picking up the kettle where Snappy was resting, Kimmi started swimming quickly around the cave. Kimmi's tail, moving up and down, propelled her swiftly through the water, but she was able to hold the kettle level in front of her. "Does this bother you?" She called out as she swam down the hall.

Keeping his head inside of the kettle, Snappy wasn't buffeted by the current as Kimmi swam around. "This works!" Snappy replied happily. "Where to now?"

"Well, one of my chores is to go to our garden to pick some fresh seaweed for dinner. Are you ready to go to the garden?" Kimmi asked.

"Yes!" he answered without hesitation. "This will be fun!"

Keeping only the top of his head above the kettle rim, Snappy was able to see where they were going, while not getting caught in the current, as Kimmi swam full speed out of the cave. Kimmi was careful to hold the kettle in front of her using both hands as she swam toward the garden. She also peeked at Snappy frequently, making sure he was still there.

Once they got to the garden, Kimmi realized she had forgotten the gathering mat, and turned sharply to swim back to get it, tipping the kettle almost halfway over as they headed back to her cave.

"Kimmi, be careful!" Snappy called out in a panic, trying to stay inside the kettle. "I am falling out!"

Glancing down, Kimmi saw him struggling to stay inside the kettle and quickly held it straight up again, where he was safe from having the current—or gravity—pull him out. She realized he could fall out if she kept swimming like this, and who knows where he would end up?

"That was close!" Snappy called out cautiously. "We will have to be more careful if we go out like this again."

"Agreed," Kimmi responded with a serious voice, suddenly realizing that she had almost lost her charge—and it was her job to keep him safe!

"Okay, let me get my gathering mat, and then we can go back." Holding the kettle in front of her with both hands, she swam back to the cave. Once she grabbed the mat, she headed back to the garden. Holding the mat in one hand and the kettle in front of her in the other hand, she constantly checked to make sure Snappy was safe. She could see the top of his head sticking out over the rim of the kettle, just far enough so he could see where they were going.

The gathering mat she held was made of strong seaweed stems that had been woven together to make a large square and was a little shorter than Kimmi was in height. She would unroll the mat and gather the dinner greens and put them on top of the mat; then roll the mat together to carry their harvest back to the caves.

Once among the various seaweed and kelp varieties in the garden, she put the mat on the ground and set the kettle with Snappy down next to it. Then she turned her attention to picking a few leaves from each stem. She followed the rules and made sure she only took two or three leaves from each plant so it could continue to grow and be healthy.

Kimmi gave her full attention to her task, and after a few minutes she had moved down the kelp row and was several feet away from Snappy. She looked at her gathering mat and smiled, as it was almost full.

"Just a few more minutes, Snappy," she called out as she picked a few additional leaves. "We shall have a delicious dinner tonight!"

However, Snappy didn't want to stay still while Kimmi filled the mat, and he looked around at what else he could do to pass the time. There were some interesting rocks only a few yards away. He glanced over at Kimmi, whose full attention was on her harvest duties. Then Snappy swam out of the kettle, and he was immediately caught by the current and was being pushed away from Kimmi! The current was strong; he could not fight against the water carrying him away from Kimmi and the kelp garden.

"Kimmi, help!" he called out to her as he struggled with the current, getting farther and farther away.

"What's the matter, Snappy?" she replied as she turned to the kettle and realized he wasn't there! "Where are you, Snappy?" she yelled as she grabbed the kettle.

Chapter Five

Broken Necklace

"I'm over here!" Snappy called out.

Swimming rapidly over to him, she scooped Snappy up with the kettle and put her hand over the top so he wouldn't fall out.

Holding the kettle with Snappy close to her as she grabbed the gathering mat, she asked, "What happened, Snappy? Why did you get out of the kettle? You knew it was keeping you safe!"

"I wanted to explore," he replied, trying to explain his actions. "I didn't realize I had to worry about the current if you weren't swimming. I'm sorry."

"We're both learning, Snappy, it's okay." Kimmi reassured him. "You must remember to stay in the kettle, and I learned earlier I must make sure I hold it straight up when I'm swimming—we both learned something new today! New rule, you must stay in the kettle when you are out with me, okay?"

Nodding his head, Snappy agreed. "Yes, Kimmi, I will!"

Holding the kettle in front of her with one hand and the gathering mat in the other hand, she started the trip back to the caves where the mermaids lived. She focused on keeping the kettle straight even as she moved her tail up and down, so Snappy wouldn't fall out. She also kept the kettle closer to her than it was on the way out, so she could balance it and the full gathering mat while remaining straight in the water. Because Kimmi was holding the kettle closer, her pearl necklace was hanging down in front of Snappy, and lightly tapped him on the head repeatedly. It didn't hurt, it was just a little annoying.

Snap! Snappy grabbed the pearl necklace with his new teeth and snapped, causing the necklace to break, and the pearls started falling to the seafloor below.

"Oh, Kimmi," he cried out. "I'm so sorry! I didn't mean to..."

"What's the matter?" she asked, looking down at him in the kettle. "Did you fall out? What happened?" As she looked down at him, she saw several of her pearls slipping off the thread of her necklace and heading out of sight through the water to the sea floor below.

"Snappy, what happened?!" Kimmi shouted as she started to panic. "Look at my pearl necklace—how did it break?!"

"Please don't be mad!" Snappy pleaded. "It was hitting me on the head, and I snapped at it. I didn't know it would break!"

"Okay, Snappy," Kimmi answered slowly. She felt herself getting angry and worked to get control of her emotions before she said anything else. She had to think it out—what was the problem, and what was the solution? That's what Alleana always said, think it out first!

"It was an accident," she said softly. "However, I need to get my pearl necklace back. It means a lot to me!"

Kimmi stopped to look around and get her location, she would have to come back to this exact spot to find her pearls, so she noted the rocks and coral formations. There was a large brain coral enclosed by two flat rocks below them, and she noted this spot for when they would return.

Then she spoke to Snappy, trying to be cheerful. "Snappy, let's take dinner back to the cave, and then you can help me find my pearls, okay?"

"Yes, Kimmi, I'll be glad to help find the pearls, I didn't mean to break your necklace," he said quietly. "I won't do it again, I promise."

"Snappy, we are still getting used to each other, so it's okay," she answered, realizing he didn't mean to break the necklace. "We have a lot to learn before we make a great team, remember? This is a way for us to learn more about each other."

"There may be some in the kettle!" Snappy added, trying to add some good news. "I felt some go down my back when they started falling. That's a good thing, right?"

"Yes, Snappy," Kimmi answered with a smile, then paused for a moment thinking to herself. "There were 41 pearls on the necklace," she said. "Once we get back to the cave, we can see how many are left. Then we will know how many we still need to find."

Swimming swiftly to save time, Kimmi made it back to the cave entrance in a few minutes. She left the mat full of leaves in the dining cave, and then swam to her sleeping cave.

"Okay, Snappy," she said. "Let's see how many pearls are here, and how many we need to find."

Snappy swam out of the kettle, and Kimmi turned it over onto her sandy bed. Several pearls hit the sand, each making a little plop of sand fly up. Kimmi swam close to the sand, with Snappy watching over her shoulder.

"Okay, let's count them. We were lucky, it looks like a lot fell into the kettle!" Kimmi said cheerfully, counting out loud for each one she picked up. After reaching the number 23, she stopped. "Well, it looks like we have 23 pearls, so we need to find the 18 we lost, right?"

"Okay, how do we do that?" Snappy said, looking at the small pile of pearls in Kimmi's hand.

"Well, it's several hours until we are expected back. If we sneak out now, we can find the rest of my pearls, we should be all done before dinner, right?" Kimmi asked, looking at Snappy.

Nodding his head, Snappy agreed. "Okay, let's find your pearls!" Then he swam over to the kettle and settled back in, only his eyes peeking out over the top.

Kimmi nodded back, took the handle of the kettle in both hands, and headed back out toward the garden. "Let's go!"

Chapter Six

LOST AND FOUND

As she got closer to where the pearls fell, Kimmi slowed down, looking all around her. She wanted to stop exactly where she remembered the pearls slipping off her necklace. Remembering there were two flat rocks with a large brain coral in between, she looked for that arrangement.

As she traced her way back in her mind, Snappy called out to her. "Look, Kimmi, it looks like some of your pearls on top of that rock!" Snappy's head popped out of the kettle and several of Snappy's appendages were waving toward one of the rocks below.

"I see them!" Kimmi shouted as she headed rapidly down to the rock, tilting the kettle as she went.

"Remember to hold the kettle up!" Snappy reminded her as he crouched farther back in the kettle so as not to fall out.

"Oh, right! Sorry!" Kimmi said, righting the kettle while still swimming down to pick up the pearls. "Look, there are seven here, that is great! Only 11 pearls left!"

"Kimmi," Snappy called. "You can store the pearls at the bottom of the kettle, then we won't lose them, okay?"

"Great idea, Snappy!" Kimmi replied, putting the seven pearls into the kettle.

"Look, there may be a few on that coral!" Kimmi shouted as she swam toward a coral growth. "Keep your eyes open, and we should be able to find them all!"

"I will!" Snappy said, glad they were able to find Kimmi's pearls.

Scooping up the pearls with her hand, Kimmi counted them. "There are five more!" she exclaimed. "I'll put these in the kettle with the others!"

"Let's look on the other rock over there, this is where I remember them falling!" Kimmi called to Snappy as she headed toward a smaller rock. "We only need to find six more!"

Suddenly, Kimmi stopped swimming. "What's that?" she asked in a hushed voice, looking out into the deeper water beyond the coral.

Quickly hiding behind a rock and keeping Snappy close to her, they watched as a creature swam in front of them, barely visible in the shadows of the water about 40 feet away. It was larger than a mermaid, but its tail was doing something strange. It didn't flap up and down like a mermaid, it looked like it was split into two pieces, each side kicking separately up and down.

"Oh no," Kimmi said softly. "It looks like its tail is broken! Let's make sure it gets home!"

But Snappy wasn't so ready to follow this creature. "Have you seen anything like that before?" Snappy asked. "I'm afraid of getting too far away from the caves. Is it safe to get any closer? What if it decides to eat us?" His voice was full of fear of the unknown, he hadn't been out into open water without his parents to protect him before.

"It will be okay, we will hide. It won't see us!" Kimmi said confidently. "I want to make sure it can swim home. Alleana says we are here to help the sea creatures! And like you said, what if something else sees it swimming so awkwardly, they may decide it looks like dinner!"

"Oh, okay," Snappy said reluctantly. "But only if we don't let it see us. We need to be sure to hide so it doesn't know we are watching it. And only for a little bit, remember you still have six more pearls to find before dinner!"

"You're right," Kimmi replied, thinking for a few seconds before continuing. "We do need to find those pearls. How about we make sure it gets to the safety of the rocks over there, and then we will return to find the rest of the pearls. Is that okay?"

"Okay, we can do that!" Snappy said, feeling a little better that they weren't going out into deeper water.

"Deal!" Kimmi said as she came out from behind the rock, not wanting to lose sight of this creature who might need their help. They followed it for a short while when it stopped and swam down to a section of coral. It looked at the area surrounding the coral for a few minutes and then continued toward the open water.

"Wait a minute, what is on the coral where it stopped?" Kimmi asked. As the creature got farther away, she swam over to the coral to see what caught its attention.

"Oh, no, look!" she exclaimed. "Something has fallen onto the coral and has broken some of its branches. We must get it off! Alleana says coral must be able to get the light that shines from above the water!"

"Maybe we should go back for help," Snappy suggested. "It seems like things are getting a little out of hand for you and me."

"No, no, we will be fine," Kimmi said assuredly. "I will push this thing off the coral, so it can get sunlight and heal itself."

Kimmi swam over to the coral and put the kettle with Snappy inside down on a rock nearby. "Now, Snappy, remember not to leave the kettle, okay?"

"I won't, I know better now. What are you going to do?" he asked. "Don't get hurt, okay?"

"Don't worry, I will figure it out," she said as she pushed on the object. She wasn't sure what it was, but she needed to move it from the coral!

Chapter Seven

WHAT IS THAT?

The object on top of the coral was shaped like a large square, about half as long as Kimmi and had a height of the length of her arm from her elbow to her hand. Maybe it was another type of container for carrying things that had fallen from the other world, like the kettle. But it didn't matter now, she needed to get it off the coral.

Kimmi was just learning about coral, and she remembered Alleana telling her they needed to have sunlight to survive. Coral, Alleana had explained, was sort of a mix between a plant and an animal. It ate little sea bugs, but also was home to algae that grew food using sunlight filtered through the water from above. This container was blocking the coral from getting the light it needed!

After a few pushes, she was able to get the big container to fall off the coral onto the sandy sea bottom below.

"There!" she said. "That should help the coral." She looked next to the container and saw several small pieces of coral had broken off and were laying on the sand. She wasn't sure what she should do with them, so she picked the pieces up and put them on a rock next to the coral; maybe they could attach to the rocks and grow there. She wasn't sure, though, and wanted to check with Alleana on what to do with broken coral pieces.

"Okay, now, back to our quest—do you see where the creature went?" Kimmi asked as she swam back to Snappy.

"I don't see it now, but it looked like it was swimming to that wide open area." Snappy answered, concern sneaking back into his voice. "I'm not sure if it is safe for a hurt creature to be swimming there, and I'm not sure if we should be going there either. Maybe we should head toward home," he suggested, and attempting get her attention away from this creature he added, "Remember the pearls!"

Kimmi was not listening to Snappy; she was too focused on following the creature. There were no rocks or coral to hide behind, nothing but open water. Kimmi swam close to the bottom, so she wouldn't be so noticeable; however, her red hair was waving back and forth with the sea currents as she swam, she wasn't hiding well with a full head of hair surrounding her! She remembered Alleana sometimes tied her hair back with the seaweed stems. She would have to try that sometime!

"Kimmi," he started. "I don't think this is a good idea. My mom said not to swim in open areas, it is very dangerous. That's where the big fish swim, and some are not so friendly." Snappy popped his head out of the kettle and turned to look at Kimmi, his eyes staring into hers, trying to get her attention. In a nervous voice he asked, "Can we go home now?"

"We will be fine," Kimmi said as she peered into the water in front of them. She wasn't afraid of the open water, knowing mermaids can outswim almost any creature in the ocean.

"Oh, look, I see it! Let's go!" Snappy ducked back into the kettle as Kimmi grabbed it and started swimming swiftly out into the open area.

"Just a few more minutes, I promise!" Kimmi replied. "Look, it is swimming toward the big rock formation in the middle of the open water. You know, I don't remember that rock being there before." For the first time, Kimmi was not sure they should be swimming this far away from the pod.

"Kimmi," Snappy said, his voice more insistent. "Maybe we should head back now. If you don't remember the rock there before, then something is wrong."

Kimmi stopped swimming, held the kettle close to her, and whispered to Snappy, "Let's see what happens, I won't get any closer, agreed?" She didn't want her young charge to be scared, and she was also starting to worry about exactly what was going on. "We can watch from here."

"Agreed," Snappy responded. "We don't need to get any closer!"

As they watched, the creature swam to the top of the tall rock, reached out and opened the side of the rock and swam inside. This made no sense—how can you swim inside a rock? Kimmi started swimming closer, she had to figure this one out.

"Kimmi!" Snappy whispered urgently. "You said no closer, remember? We agreed!"

"Just a little closer, I need to see what's going on over there!" Kimmi responded, her curiosity kept pulling her closer, she had to know what this was and how it could get inside a rock!

As they got closer to the rock formation, she saw some parts of the walls of the rock were clear, and there was some type of light shining from inside! Kimmi and Snappy watched, fascinated with the scene unfolding before them. This creature appeared to be taking off items of clothing, including taking the fins off his broken tail! What was this strange creature?

Now Kimmi was concerned, and wanted to get all the information she could, so she could report it to Alleana. Alleana always said to tell her if anything new or out of the ordinary was happening. This activity fit into that category!

"Snappy, we will need to make a report to Alleana about this creature and the rock with clear sides and shiny lights inside of it," Kimmi whispered. "Let's observe for a few more minutes and then we will get back to the caves." Almost to herself, she continued, "I wonder if I can get any closer."

"Don't go any closer, Kimmi!" Snappy said urgently.

Chapter Eight

SOMETHING DIFFERENT

"We don't know what's going on! It could be dangerous!" Snappy continued, trying to get Kimmi to turn around and head back to the caves. "My mother always told me to leave this type of situation where you don't know what is happening. Find someone older to discuss it with, as they probably have the knowledge to respond correctly. Let's go home!"

Kimmi was not listening though and was already heading toward the large rock with the lights. "Just a little closer!" she whispered to Snappy as she stared at the rock. Snappy slipped down into the kettle so he couldn't be seen from the outside.

Swimming in the open water, the silvery-blue color of Kimmi's skin and her light blue tail blended into the many hues of blue in the water, so she was almost invisible. Almost. Her hair was like a beacon, ruby red and in vivid contrast to the various blue tones of the water surrounding them.

"Okay, Snappy," Kimmi whispered as she stopped swimming to the rock. "This is far enough. Let's watch to see what happens, so we can give a full report to Alleana!"

Watching in silence, they saw the creature, now without any fins on its feet, start moving upright around inside the clear wall of the rock. It moved back and forth between different points, picking something up, putting it somewhere else. Looking around, it finally walked up to the edge of the clear wall of rock, and it stared out to look into the water beyond.

Kimmi tried to stay motionless, but she couldn't help that her hair was swaying with the current. While most of her blended in completely with the sea, her hair was giving her position away! She needed to get away, but would moving make her more noticeable?

"Snappy," she whispered to him. "It may be able to see us, because of my hair!" She was starting to panic now; she did not want to be seen by this strange creature who could take the fins off its tail.

"What if you remain as still as possible and try to drift with the current?" Snappy suggested. "It looks like the current is heading away from the strange rock place, and it will pull you with it. Maybe you can drift out of its sight, but you won't have to swim or draw any attention to yourself."

Kimmi looked at Snappy and realized he was trying to find a way out of their current dilemma. She also realized he was sitting in a black kettle, another item that would stand out against the muted blue colors of the water and sand. He was also visible to this creature!

"Great idea, Snappy!" Kimmi replied. "Maybe I can drift to those rocks, so there won't be any reason for it to look out here anymore. Okay, here we go!"

Leaning back slightly but making sure to keep the opening of kettle faced upwards, Kimmi tried to relax and let the current carry her away. She could feel the current take hold, and slowly they were drifting toward a rocky overhang and away from the scary rock structure with the creature staring out the clear walls.

As she drifted, she looked over to the clear rock wall, and saw the creature was staring right back at her! They had been seen!

That was enough for Kimmi, they had to get out of there and now! She turned and started swimming as fast as she could toward the rocks and away from the scary rock structure in the middle of the open area. "Hold on Snappy!" she called to him. "We are going to get to shelter as fast as we can! Maybe it didn't see us!"

She wanted to keep Snappy calm, but Kimmi was panicking inside. Whatever it was inside the glass wall, it had seen her—carrying a black kettle—and swimming against the current. What should they do now? Should they report it? The standing rule was to report any unusual incidents directly to Alleana as soon as possible.

But Kimmi wasn't supposed to be there and wasn't supposed to take Snappy off the reef. Maybe they don't tell Alleana? She would think about it once they were in the safety of the caves. For now, Kimmi concentrated on the immediate problem—getting home—they could worry about everything else later!

Swimming close to the rocks and coral reefs, Kimmi headed straight for the home caves. Making sure to always hold the kettle level and checking on Snappy every few seconds, they made it back to the cave opening and went inside.

"Alleana," she called out. "I have something to report. Are you here?" There was no answer.

Swimming into the main meeting cave where they first met the sea dragons, she called out again. "Alleana, where are you?"

"Here I am," Alleana replied with concern as she swam into the meeting cave from one of the small caves. "What has happened? Is Snappy okay?"

"Yes, Alleana, Snappy is fine—he was never in any danger," Kimmi started. She paused for a moment, trying to figure out what to report.

Chapter Nine

Reporting the Discovery

"I need to report an incident to you, like you told me," Kimmi was talking quickly, trying to let Alleana know what they saw. "We saw a strange creature with a broken tail swimming near the edge of the reef. We saw it go into a big rock with a clear side, and there were lights inside the rock. We also saw a big container sitting on top of a bed of coral, and I pushed it into the sand to help the coral get some light." Kimmi then paused to see what Alleana's response would be to her report.

"Kimmi, where did you see the container? And where did you see this creature? I thought we told you and all the mermaids not to go beyond the reef. Did you go beyond the coral reef today?" Alleana asked, wondering what Kimmi had been up to, hoping she had been keeping the safety of her charge, Snappy, as her top priority.

Kimmi started talking quickly again, trying to explain. "Well, Snappy and I went out to harvest some greens for dinner. On the way back my necklace broke, so we brought the greens back to the dining cave and went back to find the pearls that had gotten lost."

Snappy looked at Kimmi. "Yes, Kimmi is correct," Snappy added in support of her report, relieved Kimmi hadn't brought up the fact he was the one who broke the necklace! "We went back to where the pearls had fallen and found several scattered on a rock, and that is where we saw the creature with the broken tail!"

"So you were still on the reef, and in between the gardens and the caves." Alleana said and gave a sigh of relief. "That is good, thank you, Kimmi, for following my directions and staying within the reef." Alleana replied, glad Kimmi was finally following her instructions. "Now tell me about this creature with a broken tail, what was wrong with its tail?"

"Well..." Kimmi started, and then paused, tried to think of how to explain it. "Well, you know how we swoosh our tails up and down, one big movement at a time? This creature looked like its tail was broken in two, so half went up while the other half went down. It was something I have never seen before, have you?"

"Kimmi," Alleana said, the concern returned in her voice. "What did you do next? Did you let this creature see you?"

"I was worried about it and wanted to make sure it got home safely. It wasn't moving very fast with the broken tail. So, we did follow it a little beyond the reef. And then it did something even more surprising—it went to a large rock, opened the side of the rock, and went inside. And the rock had clear walls and there were lights inside." Kimmi paused, not sure how much she would reveal.

"One more thing," she added. "We could see it through the clear wall, and it looked like it took the fins off its broken tail! We left to come home after we saw that. I knew we had to report it to you, like you said to do." Kimmi stopped again, not wanting to add the creature may have seen her and Snappy outside of the clear wall.

"Yes, Kimmi," Alleana replied. "Thank you for telling me this. It is very important you do not go beyond the reef for this very reason. Remember, you are in charge of Snappy, to make sure he is fed, gets his sleep, and most importantly to protect him. We cannot put him in any danger, right?"

"Yes, Alleana, I understand," said Kimmi softly, and nodded her head, she was glad they made it back safely.

"Snappy, are you okay?" Alleana asked, looking at him, his head was peeking out of the kettle. "And ... that is an interesting container, why are you in it?"

"Yes, Alleana," Snappy answered. "I am fine. Kimmi and I are learning how to work together to be a team. Kimmi and I figured out how to swim together. She carries me in the kettle, and she holds it carefully, so I don't fall out. This way I can go with her to harvest dinner and look for her pearls."

"Yes," Alleana replied, hesitating for a moment. "About those pearls. I'm sorry Kimmi, but it is too dangerous for you and Snappy to go back out to find the rest of the pearls. Especially with this creature with the broken tail swimming around the area. Why don't you and Snappy get a little rest before dinner, you have both had a long and very exciting first day!"

"But my pearls are on the reef, not in the open water!" Kimmi pleaded, hoping to change Alleana's mind, she felt an urgent need to get the rest of her pearls. "We will stay on the reef and not go out to the big rock, I promise!"

"No, Kimmi," Alleana replied with a firm voice, explaining why Kimmi could not go looking for her pearls.

"Kimmi, remember your main job is taking care of Snappy, and it is too dangerous to take him back to the reef today, especially with the creature swimming about."

"Okay," Kimmi said softly, looking at Snappy. Although she tried to smile, it was a sad smile, and her eyes showed her disappointment at not being able to go back to the reef to find the missing pearls.

"Could she go if I promise to stay in her sleeping cave?" Snappy asked. "Then I will be sure to be safe!" Snappy felt sad too, knowing it was his fault her necklace had broken in the first place.

"No, Snappy," Alleana replied. "Kimmi is responsible for you, and she has promised your parents she will always be with you. We must keep our promises, that is how we build trust with our friends."

Chapter Ten

BACK AGAIN

Alleana saw how anxious Kimmi was, her eyes wide and her lips trembling. Kimmi needed to get her pearls, even if she didn't know where they came from. Kimmi had an emotional connection with the pearls Alleana had never seen before. Maybe it was because Kimmi was the first mermaid Alleana had seen who was transformed into a mermaid with a human necklace. No other mermaids in Alleana's pod had any human belongings with them after their transformation.

Turning to Kimmi, Alleana reached out her hands and took Kimmi's hands in hers. Looking into her eyes, Alleana said, "Kimmi, I know your necklace meant a lot to you. It was the one thing you had from the before time. Once we resolve the issue about this creature you saw, I promise the other mermaids and I will look for your pearls. If we can't find them, we will help you find enough pearls to remake your necklace with the ones you and Snappy found. It is too dangerous right now to go out. I am sorry."

"I understand, Alleana," Kimmi replied softly. "And thank you for saying you will help me remake my pearl necklace once this mystery is solved." Kimmi had been with Alleana since she could remember and knew Alleana was doing what was best. As the leader of the pod, Alleana had chosen to be Kimmi's mentor, to teach her what she needed to know to be a good mermaid, always taking the time to make sure Kimmi was safe every night.

Picking up the kettle containing Snappy, Kimmi slowly turned to swim to her cave. "We will go take a quick nap before dinner like you suggested, Alleana, and Snappy can try out his new bed." Kimmi's voice was a bit more cheerful as she looked at Snappy and said, "How does that sound, Snappy?"

Snappy looked up at her and replied, "Yes, Kimmi, that sounds like a good idea, it has been a very busy day today! Thank you for keeping me safe!"

"Okay, that's what we will do, we make a great team!" Kimmi said, getting her enthusiasm back as she smiled at Snappy, she was still on an adventure and had a new friend!

"We will see you at dinner!" Kimmi called to Alleana as she swam toward her sleeping cave, making sure to keep the kettle level for Snappy.

Once back at the cave, Kimmi took Snappy over to the seaweed bed she made for him. "Why don't you try this out and get comfortable. There's time for a quick nap before dinner okay, Snappy?"

However, instead of getting out of the kettle and into the seaweed, Snappy looked back at Kimmi and suggested, "Why don't we go look for your pearls for a few minutes before dinner. It was my fault the necklace broke, and I am so sorry you lost your pearls."

"What?" Kimmi exclaimed, surprised by the suggestion. "Didn't you hear what Alleana said? I can't go anywhere without you, and it will be too dangerous for me to take you out to the reef with me to hunt for my pearls."

"Yes, but what if I want to go look for the pearls?" Snappy asked. "You wouldn't be taking me while you looked for pearls, you would be accompanying me!" Snappy's big eyes looked into hers, wanting to let her know he wanted to help her get her pearls back.

"Does that make sense? Okay, I'm not looking for my pearls, but you are, and I am staying with you while you look for them?" Kimmi was getting confused at this point. "But doesn't your plan have me taking you back out to the reef where we saw the creature?"

"Well," Snappy countered. "You will be accompanying me to protect me." Swimming out of the kettle, he slowly started to the entrance to the cave. "See, I'm going, and you are going to make sure I am safe. I will tell Alleana I was the one who made the decision, and you wanted to stay with me to keep me safe, like you promised."

"Okay, Snappy," Kimmi said, still a little confused. "I will go with you to keep you safe, like I promised!"

Once the decision was made, it only took Kimmi and Snappy a few minutes to get back to the place where her necklace broke. Swimming to the rock where they found the first seven pearls, Kimmi asked, "Okay, Snappy, where should we look next?"

"Let's dig in the sand below the rock, Kimmi," Snappy replied. "Maybe they rolled off. If we had waited until tomorrow the changing tides would have buried them or shifted the sand where they are hidden. That's what I was thinking."

"I'll look there, Snappy!" Kimmi exclaimed, "Good thinking on your part!"

Swimming to the bottom of the rock, Kimmi set the kettle with Snappy next to her, and she ran her fingers through the sand like a rake, trying to locate the pearls. After a few minutes, she made a fist and pulled her hand out of the sand.

"Snappy, you are right!" she called out as she held up a pearl. "And look, it has the little hole where the string held it together, this is one of my pearls!"

"I'm so glad, Kimmi," Snappy answered happily. "Are there any more?"

Moving a little farther from the rock, she started running her fingers through the sand again. "Yes!" Kimmi exclaimed as she held up her hand to show two more pearls. "Two more!"

As Kimmi reached over to put them in the kettle, she noticed movement near the coral where she had knocked off the container, there were more creatures swimming around!

"Snappy," she whispered urgently as she grabbed the kettle and headed back to the caves, "we need to go back now! The creatures are back!"

"Okay," Snappy replied. "Let's go!"

Chapter Eleven

RESPONSIBILITY

Kimmi swam rapidly, wanting to get back to the safety of the caves. At least this time she hadn't been seen!

"Made it!" she whispered as she and Snappy slipped back into her cave.

Swimming over to Snappy's seaweed bed, she held the kettle close so he could swim into the seaweed. As he was getting settled in, Kimmi swam over and rested in her bed.

"Okay," Kimmi whispered. "Remember we were taking a nap!"

A few minutes later, Alleana swam into the room.

"I'm glad to see you are back, Kimmi," she said calmly as she swam over. "Where were you? I came to check on you and Snappy a while ago, and you were not here."

Snappy poked his face out of the seaweed. "It was me, Alleana!" he said. "I told her I would find her pearls. She stayed with me to keep me safe. She was going to stay in the cave, but she wanted to protect me."

"Kimmi," Alleana said sternly as she turned to look at her. "What really happened?"

Kimmi looked at Snappy, thinking hard at what to answer, it had been so confusing earlier. "Well, Snappy said he was going to find my pearls. He was sad I had lost them. He started swimming out of the cave, and I stayed with him, so he would not get hurt."

"So it was not your idea?" Alleana asked.

"No, Alleana, it was my idea," Snappy answered before Kimmi could reply. "What Kimmi didn't tell you was I was the one who broke the necklace. She didn't get mad at me, and I wanted to make sure she got her pearls back, because I was the one who lost them."

"Kimmi," Alleana asked, this time in a softer tone. "Is that true?"

"Yes, Alleana," Kimmi replied softly. "When we were coming back from the garden, Snappy snapped at my necklace. He bit it and broke the string, sending the pearls flying all over. We found three more pearls a few minutes ago, so we have now found all but three of them."

"Okay, thank you both for telling me the truth," Alleana replied. "Now, let's look at what happened, and what shouldn't have happened, okay? This will be another learning experience on being a great team."

Turning to look at Snappy, Alleana spoke quietly, "Snappy, that was good of you to be concerned for Kimmi's necklace. However, you would not be able to make it to the reef yourself. You asked Kimmi to go with you, so you could look for the pearls. You asked Kimmi to do something I told her not to do. Snappy, you need to understand we have promised to keep you safe, so you must let Kimmi and I decide what is best, okay?"

"Yes, Alleana," Snappy replied, realizing his mistake. "I know you didn't want Kimmi to go to the reef, but I convinced her it would be okay. I'm sorry."

"Thank you, Snappy. I'm glad you now realize it is very important to us that we keep you safe, we have promised your parents, and we must keep our promises, okay?" Alleana said.

As Snappy nodded his head in understanding, Alleana then turned to Kimmi.

"Kimmi," Alleana said softly. "I know you were trying to do what is right, but you must listen to me when I tell you something. Even if Snappy wanted to go, he could not have gone to look for the pearls without you. He could not swim fast enough. Please make sure you think about all the facts surrounding a matter before making a decision that could result in someone getting hurt, okay? Remember, think it out first, right?"

"Yes, Alleana," Kimmi replied, realizing she should have told Snappy they could not go, even if he wanted to do so, like Alleana told her not to go. That would be the right thing to do. "I will be more responsible with Snappy, and make sure he is safe, whether he agrees or not, I promise I will think first!"

"Thank you, Kimmi," Alleana answered with a smile. "I am glad you are learning responsibility; it is very important to keep your promises, especially when it comes to Snappy's safety." As Alleana turned to leave Kimmi's sleeping cave, she called back, "Why don't you both go to the dining cave and get some of the leaves you picked earlier, and then you can return here for the night."

"Yes, Alleana," Kimmi said. "That sounds like a good idea!"

Alleana was almost outside the cave when Kimmi called her back.

"Alleana," Kimmi called to her. "I do need to tell you one more thing."

"Yes, Kimmi?" she said as she turned around, wondering what else Kimmi wanted to say.

"Alleana, while we were out looking for the rest of the pearls, there were more creatures over by the container I knocked off the coral." Kimmi was very serious, knowing Alleana would need to know this to protect all the mermaids. "I came back as soon as I saw them."

"Thank you, Kimmi," Alleana replied with concern. "I will let the other mermaids know. Please remember not to go out near where your necklace dropped again, okay?"

"Yes, Alleana, I will remember this time!" Kimmi said with enthusiasm, she would do her best to keep Snappy safe!

Chapter Twelve

SAFETY FIRST!

Kimmi and Snappy had a restful night, sleeping in their comfortable beds until the light returned to the sleeping cave. Alleana swam into the cave and woke them up, getting them ready to start another busy day.

"Good morning, sleepyheads!" Alleana called out. "Remember, every morning you have to gather the greens for dinner."

"Good morning, Alleana," Kimmi replied sleepily. "We will go in a few minutes. Let me wake up first, okay?"

"Of course, Kimmi, no rush," Alleana answered. "I wanted to make sure you go to the southern kelp garden today, since we are having unknown creatures visiting the area of the main garden. Is that okay with you? Do you remember how to get there?"

A little more awake, Kimmi took a moment to think before answering.

"Yes, Alleana," she replied. "We go through the south cave entrance and past the large coral reef on the right. Just past the coral is our southern garden. Is that right?"

"Good job, Kimmi, you are exactly right!" Alleana said with pride, smiling at Kimmi.

Kimmi was glad the daily training she had been receiving was coming back to her. Alleana had been giving Kimmi lessons daily on various topics, how to find the gardens, how to give a mermaid siren, how to tell a friendly fish from one not so friendly, and never to go into open water alone. There were so many things Kimmi would have to remember to be safe in her pod. There was even more to remember now that she was in charge of Snappy's safety also.

Kimmi smiled back at Alleana, glad Alleana was proud of her. Then she swam over to where Snappy was resting and called to him, "Wake up Snappy! We are going to the south garden today! Time to wake up!" She moved the seaweed around, trying to find him, his camouflage was very effective!

"Good morning, Kimmi and Alleana!" Snappy said as he poked his head out of the seaweed. "I'm ready for another fun day!"

"Let's hope it won't be as eventful as yesterday, okay?" Alleana said as she smiled at Snappy, her voice revealing her concern. "You both should hope for a nice quiet day, right?"

"Yes, Alleana," Kimmi said, a little disappointed they weren't going to be going on an explore or doing something exciting. She realized, though, to keep her promise to the sea dragons, she had to keep Snappy safe at all costs, even if it meant having boring days gathering kelp together. "We will try to have a nice, quiet day."

Swimming slowly out of his seaweed bed, Snappy headed toward Kimmi.

"Kimmi, we will still use the kettle, right?" he asked.

"Yes, of course!" Kimmi replied happily. At least it was fun for Snappy. She would make sure he had a fun ride in the kettle on their way to and from the south garden.

"Oh," Snappy added. "Don't forget to bring the gathering mat this time!"

"You're right, Snappy!" Kimmi answered. "I forgot it last time, didn't I? Well, let's get it from the dining cave and be on our way! Thanks for reminding me. We do make a good team, don't we?"

"We make a great team! Thanks for helping me learn to be a good sea dragon!" Snappy said. "I'm glad you are watching out for me!"

Heading out the south cave, Snappy stuck his head out of the kettle and looked around. Another new place to see! Keeping only his eyes above the rim, he enjoyed moving fast as Kimmi swam past the coral reef and into the large kelp garden in front of them. It was not quite as large as the north garden, but still had a lot of seaweed and kelp of many varieties. He liked the different colors of the different plants; it reminded him of his own camouflage and why he was able to blend in so well.

"Here we are, Snappy!" Kimmi called out when they were entering the garden. The seaweed was tall, at least 20 feet long and swaying with the current. Soon they were lost in row after row of kelp.

"This should be good," Kimmi said as she put the kettle on the ground next to the gathering mat. "Now, remember, you can't get out of the kettle, right?"

"Yes, Kimmi, I promise!" Snappy replied, remembering the last time he tried to sneak out to explore his surroundings.

Spending a few moments peering down the rows of kelp with Snappy, Kimmi pointed out one side of the garden row opened into the blue waters beyond. Large schools of fish swam by, and occasionally a turtle would swim through the kelp bed. She thought this won't be so boring for Snappy after all!

It only took a few minutes for Kimmi to get the gathering mat full, and she turned her attention back to Snappy. "Okay, Snappy, are you ready to head back?"

But Snappy's attention was focused on something he was watching at the end of the row, and he didn't respond.

"Snappy, are you okay?" Kimmi asked, getting closer to him, and then she turned to look at what he was staring at.

Kimmi stopped and looked at what was at the end of the kelp row. She asked in a scared voice, "What is that?"

"I don't know," Snappy said slowly, he was afraid also. "It is coming our way, and it is between us and the caves. What do we do now?"

Grabbing the kettle with Snappy, Kimmi swam up above the garden to get a better look at the object, and then froze in place as she stared at it. She had never seen this before, and it couldn't be good.

Chapter Thirteen

A New Danger Approaches

They both stared motionless, trying to make sense at what looked like a moving wall, slowing drifting toward them. It took up all the space from the top of the water down to the sea floor. The top was held up at the surface by floating objects; the bottom of the wall was scraping the ground and churning up the sand. Stretching out as far as they could see in either direction, this object was heading their way!

She remembered Alleana had warned her of these, but she never believed they existed. It was a ghost net, a net that floats free, catching anything in its path. Kimmi watched the ground as the ghost net was approaching. It dragged on the ground, cutting plants and toppling rocks, breaking coral branches, trapping crabs and catching anything in its path.

"Snappy," Kimmi yelled, as she snapped out of the daze of watching it move closer and closer. "I've got to get you to safety! I know what this is!"

"What, Kimmi? What is it?" Snappy asked in a scared voice, wanting to know what they were facing.

"It is a ghost net, dangerous and there's no escape if you get caught!" Kimmi said, almost in a panic, trying to keep her wits about her. What did Alleana say to do? They had discussed different things she needed to know and what to do in case it happened, and this was one of them —a ghost net!

"We need to let the pod know first, then I need to get you to safety." Kimmi was running Alleana's instructions through her head—what to do if you see this coming your way. "Okay, first let the pod know, I can do that!"

"Cover your ears, Snappy," Kimmi said as she looked at him. "This will be loud!"

"Okay, Kimmi, ready!" Snappy replied as he moved several of his camouflage appendages to surround his head.

Kimmi thought hard, she had to get this right. She had only practiced a few times in one of the caves. She swam up until she was half-way between the top of the water and the sea floor, then she called out in a siren voice, "Help! Help is needed. Please come now!"

The mermaid voice when used as a siren, was not melodic or soft, it was piercing, and would travel for miles in the water. She turned the other way and repeated the loud call. Then she swam down with Snappy to the sea floor, how could she protect him against this moving wall?

Kimmi looked around, there must be a cave or something they can hide in. She saw several rocks near the coral reef and swam over to them, looking for an entrance, somewhere they could go to for protection. She saw a small cave, big enough for the kettle with Snappy, but she would not fit in. She needed to protect him, that was her responsibility, so she would use it!

"Snappy," Kimmi called out as she swam to the small cave. "You need to stay inside this cave, inside the kettle, and not come out, okay?"

"But Kimmi, what about you?" Snappy asked, realizing she would not fit into the small cave.

"I need to keep you safe, that is my responsibility, so that is what I am going to do," Kimmi replied resolutely, she would not let Snappy get hurt! "You are small and will get caught in the net. I am remembering the next step to do with a ghost net now, and I can start as soon as you are safe."

"What are you going to do, Kimmi?" Snappy said. "I don't want you to get hurt!"

"Snappy, if you are safe, I can start cutting the net, it is what is done when one of these comes through—the mermaids gather and cut the float pieces off the top of the net that are keeping it vertical; then it will sink to the sea floor. Then we bury it to protect the other sea creatures." Kimmi was starting to remember the steps Alleana had instructed her to do in case this happened. "I know there is more, but the first step is to cut the floats from the net. I cannot do this until you are safe!"

"Okay, Kimmi ... if you are sure," Snappy responded hesitantly, very scared at this point. "Can't I stay with you?" he pleaded. "I can hide in the bottom of the kettle, and you can start cutting, will that work? Remember you aren't supposed to leave me alone anywhere!"

Looking at Snappy, Kimmi stopped to think. She could tell he didn't want to be trapped inside a small cave with the ghost net slowly approaching them. Was there a way she could keep him with her and keep him safe?

Putting the kettle on her left elbow, she practiced to see if she could still cut the lines holding the floats while holding him. It wasn't working too well. Then Kimmi remembered she was better with her left hand holding the knife, so she moved the kettle to her right elbow to try again. This time it worked better, she could keep the kettle handle on her right elbow, use her right hand to hold the net, and left hand to cut the floats off.

"Okay, Snappy, if you are sure you want to stay with me, we can do this!" Kimmi said, knowing time was running out, and they had to make their decision now.

"I will stay with you, Kimmi!" Snappy called to her as he hid in the kettle. "Let's get started!"

"Stay hidden, Snappy!" Kimmi replied nervously. "I don't want you to get accidentally caught in the net as I cut it! Please stay hidden in the kettle until I say all is clear, okay?"

"I will, Kimmi," Snappy said. "I know you can do this! I will stay hidden until you tell me I can come out. You need to be safe also! What about your hair, will it get caught?"

"You're right!" Kimmi called out. "Hold on, I'm going to get something to tie it back." Swimming back to the kelp garden, she grabbed one of the stems and used it to tie her hair back. It could be disastrous if her hair was caught in the net. "Okay, now we're ready! Let's go!"

Chapter Fourteen

FIRST LINE OF ATTACK

Swimming fast to the surface where the floats were holding up the net, Kimmi got ready to start cutting the lines. All the lines had to be cut from the floats, or the ghost net would continue to float from the surface of the water down to the bottom of the sea floor and continue to be a threat to all the sea creatures. But first she had to make sure Snappy was safe.

"Snappy," she called to him. "You need to stay totally inside the kettle, okay? Don't even stick your nose out, not until I say!"

"Yes, Kimmi, I understand. I don't want to get caught in the net!" Snappy coiled down into the kettle until all his little appendages were below the opening. "I'll keep my head down too, you don't have to worry about me!"

"Thank you, Snappy, we can do this together! I won't leave you, no matter what!" Kimmi said. Moving the handle of the kettle to her right elbow, she practiced one more time how she would hold the line with her right hand, cutting with her left hand. "Let's get started!"

Kimmi could not see the end of the net, so she started cutting the float nearest to her. It was not easy, as the line was tough, but she was able to cut through after two or three slashes with her knife.

"Okay, that's one!" Kimmi called out. "Now for the next one!"

As Kimmi went from one line to the next, she was able to see some fish and crabs caught in the net, some of them were still alive; but many had died. She was remembering what the next step was—free all the living sea creatures! However, at this point, she was the only mermaid around, so she needed to continue to cut the lines from the top, to get the net to fall onto the sea floor below and stop trapping the sea creatures. Once they got more mermaids, they would work together on a rescue mission to save anyone still alive.

Moving down the line, she saw some movement at the edge of where the net faded into the blueness. It was the creature!

She watched as it was cutting the lines also, and she nodded to it, acknowledging they were working for the same goal. As the creature continued working on cutting the lines, it nodded back to Kimmi. She watched as the creature stopped to free a large turtle who had gotten caught near it and set it free.

Kimmi was glad to have some help, this was a daunting task, and she hoped other help arrived soon! For now, it was only the two of them, strangers but with a common purpose, to save the creatures caught in the net and destroy this ghost net so it could not hurt anything else.

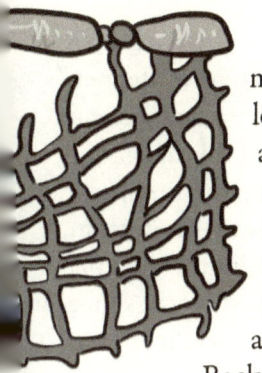

In the distance, Kimmi heard the mermaid's siren—help was on the way! Kimmi looked at the creature, and it nodded to her again, somehow knowing that was its signal to go. Maybe it knew mermaids would not appear with strange creatures around? As it turned to leave, it waved at Kimmi. She stared for a second, surprised at this action, and then she waved back. It was a friend!

Back to the cutting! Kimmi turned to the net and continued cutting the lines.

Within a few minutes Alleana arrived and swam over to her, calling out in a worried voice, "Kimmi, where is Snappy?"

"It's okay, Alleana, he is with me!" Kimmi replied. "He's hiding in the kettle. I promised I would never leave him alone, and I didn't."

"I'm in here, Alleana!" Snappy called out from inside the kettle. "Kimmi is keeping me safe!"

Reaching out to grab another line, Kimmi said to Alleana, "See, I can hold the kettle and hold a line in this hand and cut it with the other hand." She demonstrated how she had been working on the lines.

"That is good thinking, Kimmi!" Alleana replied. "Now let's get to work on this ghost net."

Alleana reached out and grabbed a line and cut through it in one slice, separating the net from the float. Kimmi could see Alleana had more experience using her knife against nets, that's why she was the leader. As she continued cutting, Alleana said, "I have heard from Sabrina's pod, and they are on their way. Once we get more mermaids to do the line cutting, I want you to work on step two, okay?"

"Yes, Alleana, I remembered step two—we need to search for and free any living creatures caught in the net." Kimmi then turned to focus on cutting lines, each one cut was another step closer to ridding the sea of this danger.

Kimmi and Alleana continued cutting the lines, and the middle of the net was starting to sag toward the bottom, with the floats holding up either side. "Kimmi," Alleana called. "You keep going that way, and I'll go this way. Once the weight of the net is mostly on the sea floor, it should stop drifting!"

"Yes, Alleana!" Kimmi replied and headed to the other side of the cut lines. "Snappy, are you still okay in there?" she asked once she was ready to start cutting again. "Don't come out, just let me know!"

Staying far inside the kettle, Snappy called out, "Yes, Kimmi, I'm fine! Keep going!"

"Okay, Snappy, thanks!" Kimmi said. "Once we get reinforcements, maybe we can work together to locate and rescue the sea creatures caught in the net!"

Kimmi continued cutting the lines on her side of the net. She and Alleana were making good progress; the net had stopped drifting, with most of its weight resting on the sea floor. Now they had to cut all the floats off the top and lay out the net, then they could search for survivors!

Chapter Fifteen

HELP ARRIVES

Soon another siren rang through the water, and three more mermaids joined Alleana and Kimmi in cutting the floats holding the net up.

"Kimmi," Alleana called to her. "Now that Sabrina and her pod have arrived, let's work together to finish your side of the net, so it is all on the ground. Then we can stretch out the net and you can start searching for survivors, okay?"

"Yes, Alleana!" Kimmi replied, glad help had arrived. She continued cutting the floats on her side and was soon joined by Sabrina and Alleana. Two other mermaids swam to the bottom of the net and started stretching it out, so it was flat on the bottom and not bunched in a pile.

"Once you have searched through the net, Sabrina's pod mates will start rolling up the net for step three!" Alleana called out. "Kimmi, you will be working with Francesca and Jessica, while I will be working with Sabrina!"

There were only a few more floats on Kimmi's side of the net, and they were speedily cut with the help of Alleana and Sabrina. As they swam to the other side of the net to start cutting the remaining floats, Kimmi swam down to the sea floor to meet the other two mermaids and start step two, the rescue!

"Greetings, Francesca and Jessica, I am Kimmi. Alleana says I should search for survivors as you are rolling up the net," Kimmi called out to them.

"Greetings, Kimmi, I'm Jessica!" Jessica called back. "Yes, please start in this corner. We will start rolling it up after it has been searched, and make sure it doesn't snag anything else while resting on the sea floor. The best way is to look at one strip of the net about the size of your outstretched hands. Please call out as you are looking, some of the creatures will be able to respond and you will find them quicker."

"Thank you, Jessica, I will do that!" Kimmi said, turning to the first area to search.

Kimmi stretched out her arms to make sure she was searching the right way and then started swimming along the length of the net. "Calling all creatures, if you can, please call to me or wiggle a fin or something, and I will come to set you free!"

"I'm over here!" called a small fish. "Please help me!"

Kimmi swam over to the fish, one of its gills was caught in the net. She carefully backed it out of the net line, making sure it didn't get hurt, and then let it go free. "Swim away, little one!" she said as she watched it swim into the water beyond.

Moving slowly over the length of the net, she found other creatures, including a small crab who was tangled inside the net and could not get out. "Please help me get untangled!" it called to her.

"Here I come!" Kimmi exclaimed as she swam over to it. She carefully cut the net, so the opening was large enough for the crab to wiggle out.

"Thank you!" the crab called as it scurried across the sea floor, looking for a safe place to hide and rest.

There were also a lot of fish and crabs that had been trapped too long and had died, and this made Kimmi distressed. She stopped swimming, trying to comprehend the magnitude of the needless destruction of these innocent lives. This ghost net had cost the lives of many creatures for no reason.

"Kimmi, what's wrong?" Snappy asked when he noticed she had stopped, and he peeked out to see she was staring at all the little creatures she could not save.

"Kimmi, you must keep going!" Snappy called to her. "Think of those you can rescue! How much it will mean to them once you have freed them!"

"Snappy," Kimmi replied, looking up and around at the net stretched before her. "You're right! My mission is to rescue every creature I can. Those that have survived need our help. We must move fast!"

Looking at Snappy in the kettle, Kimmi asked, "Snappy, do you think you could help me? Now the net is on the ground, I could use your eyes and ears to help me find the creatures that need to be rescued!"

Sticking his head out, Snappy replied, "Okay, Kimmi, I will stay in the kettle and look for the creatures, and you help them get out. I will call out to them, to make sure we get to everyone who needs our help!"

"Thank you, Snappy!" Kimmi said, relieved someone could help her find the little creatures to save and to give her encouragement to keep going. "You must stay in the kettle, but please look around and make sure I don't miss anyone!"

This arrangement worked well, as Snappy could look ahead and call out to the creatures, as Kimmi would work on getting others freed from the net. They were moving faster down the length of the net. They made it to the end of the net, and Kimmi turned around to head back, searching another section as wide as her outstretched hands.

Once they had cleared about ten feet of the net, Francesca and Jessica started rolling the ends up. The net would be in one long roll they could carry away and bury somewhere so it wouldn't hurt anyone again.

Kimmi was encouraged by all the little fish and crabs Snappy was finding; they made a great team! Snappy would find them and let Kimmi know where they were, and Kimmi would free them from the net as Snappy looked for the next one to be rescued.

It was a big net, but she wouldn't quit until it had all been checked, they would not leave anyone who needed their help!

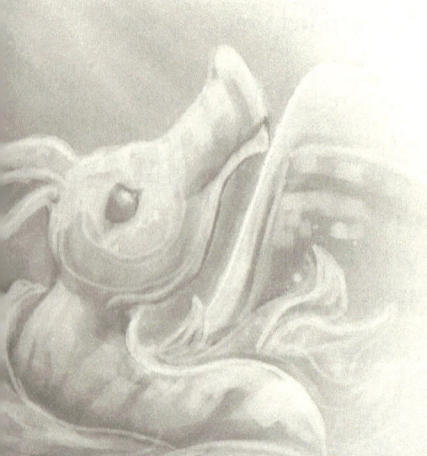

Chapter Sixteen

PROGRESS IS MADE

When all the floats had been cut and the net was laying on the sea floor, Alleana swam over to help with step two, the rescue of those trapped.

"Kimmi," Alleana called as she swam next to her. "Sabrina will be taking all the floats and throwing them out of the water. She has observed a place where the land creatures clear the beaches of the floats and debris. Once she is done, she will join us for step two. Francesca and Jessica will continue the rolling as we move along."

A few minutes later, three other members of Alleana's pod showed up, so now there were five mermaids searching for survivors!

"Greetings, my friends! Let's spread out in a long line and go through the net one section at a time; we need to rescue all who have survived," Alleana called to them.

With Alleana and the other mermaids beside her, they were making good progress, and Snappy's calls to those in need helped them identify who to rescue. It was a long net, but once everyone was helping, they would be able to complete the search and get rid of the net for good!

They were about halfway done with their search when Sabrina came back.

"Alleana," Sabrina called. "I will go find a place where we can store this net so it will no longer be a threat. I remember some caves near here, so I will see if any will be large enough to hold this net once it is rolled up."

"Good idea, Sabrina!" Alleana called back. "See if there are any rocks to weight it down close by, we do not want this one to wash back onto the sea floor!"

"I will!" Sabrina called as she swam to the south.

Swimming down her line over the net, Kimmi looked at each creature in the net, while Snappy called out to the creatures, hoping to get them to respond and move around—letting the mermaids know which ones they could rescue.

It took a while, but they did it; all parts of the net had been checked. They had been able to save hundreds of fish, big and small, along with numerous crabs and shrimp who had gotten tangled in the ghost net. Kimmi looked on that as a success, even though as many, if not more, had died after being trapped. Kimmi couldn't imagine why there would be such a creation, made for killing the sea creatures without care of what it killed.

"Alleana!" Kimmi called out. "We are ready for step three!"

"Okay, Kimmi," Alleana called back as she got closer. "We will need to move this ghost net to a place where it can never harm sea creatures again. Sabrina is out looking for a place to leave it, and then we will have to put rocks on top to keep the current from sweeping it back out onto the sea floor."

Calling to her pod, Alleana continued, "Marilyn, Suzanna, Natalie! Let's finish rolling this up, so we will be ready when Sabrina gets back, okay?"

"Yes, Alleana," Suzanne answered, and the three mermaids joined Francesca and Jessica, rolling the net as tightly as possible.

"Let's help, Kimmi," Alleana said to her, and then headed to help with rolling the net.

"On my way!" Kimmi said as she followed. "Snappy, are you good in there?"

"I am, but be careful not to tip the kettle," Snappy replied. "Sometimes you swim fast, and the kettle tips sideways, okay?"

"Yes, Snappy, of course!" Kimmi said, looking down at the kettle, making sure it was level and Snappy would not fall out. "Thank you again for helping to find the fish, I needed your help to stay focused on saving those who were still alive."

"You're welcome, Kimmi. I was glad to be of help," Snappy replied. "You will need help moving this though, hopefully you can get some larger sea creatures to assist!"

All the mermaids got together to get the final sections rolled together. Stretching about 40 feet along the sea floor, the rolled net was about three feet in diameter. This was going to be difficult to carry, even with eight mermaids!

"We need to wait for Sabrina to return, and I think I see her now," Alleana said as she searched the blue water to the south.

Getting closer, Sabrina called out to the mermaids, "I have found a large cave that will hold this net." Then she swam over to where Alleana was floating next to the net.

"This is a large net," Alleana said as Sabrina got closer. "I'm wondering if we can carry it, or if we will need help."

"I thought about that also, and I have found some friends to help us transport it to the cave," Sabrina replied. Giving a short mermaid siren call, she looked to the south.

Kimmi wondered what creature Sabrina was calling to, but she didn't have to wait long. Four giant turtles appeared out of the blue haze to the south, swimming in their direction.

"Please meet my four friends, Pauly, Tracy, Levonne, and Michael. They have graciously offered to help move this ghost net to a place where it can hurt no one else!" Sabrina called out.

As they heard their names, each turtle bowed its head to the mermaids.

"We are glad to help you rid the ocean of this death trap!" Pauly said. "Thank you for letting us be a part of your mission!"

"Thank you for your help!" Alleana called back. "It is greatly appreciated!"

"My thoughts would be to have two mermaids with each turtle," Sabrina started. "Then we can balance the net on the turtle's back and the mermaids can keep it steady and balanced, so it does not fall. Is everyone ready?"

Chapter Seventeen

FINAL RESTING PLACE

"Let's get everyone lined up in their places next to the net, then we can pick it up at one time, okay?" Sabrina asked. "I will take the lead since I know where we are going. Levonne, why don't you and Francesca join me."

"Alleana, can you take the back? You can keep an eye on everyone and can alert me if we need to stop," She continued.

"Yes, Sabrina," Alleana answered. "I will take the back. Kimmi, why don't you come back here with Pauly and me."

"Yes, I'm here," said Kimmi as she swam next to Pauly. "I will stay on Pauly's right side so I can leave the kettle with Snappy on my right arm. Snappy, make sure you stay in the kettle, okay?"

"Yes, Kimmi, you can count on me!" Snappy replied. "I'm glad you have help to move the net." Turning to the turtle near him, he said, "Hi Pauly, I'm Snappy!"

"Hello, little Snappy!" Pauly answered. "Be safe in there!"

Alleana swam to the left side of Pauly. "Good planning, Kimmi, I'll be on this side!"

Sabrina organized the other groups. As Kimmi waited for everyone to get in position, she realized Sabrina was very organized; she must have done this before. She knew exactly what needed to happen. Kimmi hoped one day she would be able to lead the mermaids like Sabrina and Alleana do and help the other sea creatures.

"Alright, team!" Sabrina called out. "Here is what will happen—and we all must follow the same steps—all the mermaids will start on the left side of the turtles, rolling the net onto their backs. Then the mermaid who is to be on the right will swim over the turtle and net and hold it from the right side. Does everyone understand?"

She paused for a moment, looking at each of the mermaids, waiting for all to nod they understood. Once all nodded, she continued.

"We will move slowly, so everyone watch those around you and move at the same pace!"

Sabrina joined Francesca on the left side of Levonne.

"Okay, position yourself next to the net and slowly start rolling it onto your turtle's back, here we go!" Sabrina called to them, as she started pushing on the net.

The net was heavy and even with all eight mermaids pushing on the net, it took a few minutes to roll it onto the backs of the turtles.

"Those on the left, hold onto the net. Those who will be on the right, swim over and get opposite your partner! Watch how we do it." Sabrina held onto her side of the net while Francesca swam to the other side. "Okay, swim over to the right!"

"Hey, Snappy!" Kimmi called to him. "We are ready to move the net, so hold on! I will do my best to keep the kettle straight!"

"Okay my friend turtles," Sabrina called to them. "Let's swim slowly, so the mermaids can keep the net balanced on your backs!"

In unison, the four turtles started swimming forward slowly and close to the sea floor. The mermaids kept their positions, one on each side, holding the net to keep it from falling off.

"It is not too far, but because we must move slowly, it will take a while." Sabrina turned to the front and kept her side balanced.

"We will need to turn to the right here, so everyone, follow my lead!" Sabrina called back. "Once we make the turn, the cave will be on the left. Keep the net balanced, we have to all turn at the same time!"

Sabrina started turning, and Levonne and Francesca followed her. The other teams did the same, and soon the net had been turned to the right. Kimmi looked to the left, trying to find the cave Sabrina referred to, where they would be leaving the net, then looked down at the kettle.

"Hey, Snappy, are you okay in there?" Kimmi asked. "It won't be too much longer now."

"I'm good, Kimmi," Snappy replied. "I'm keeping out of the way! I'm so glad you have the turtles to help, I don't think you would have been able to carry the net without them!"

"I agree!" Kimmi said. "Sabrina is very organized!"

Kimmi had taken her eyes off the net to look around and then at Snappy, and in doing so, she let go of the net, and it started shifting her way. "Snappy, hold on!" she shouted as she turned back to the net, pushing hard to get it balanced on the turtle's back again.

"Okay, everyone!" Sabrina called back. "One more turn, to the left, and then we will swim it into the cave."

Sabrina, Levonne, and Francesca slowly turned to the left and the other teams followed their actions. The cave was not too far away now, and it looked large enough to hold the net on the back of the turtles, as well as the mermaids holding it steady.

Guiding it in, Sabrina called back to Alleana. "Alleana, let me know when the net is inside, and we can stop."

Once they were inside, Alleana called out, "Sabrina, the net is inside the cave!"

"Okay, very important! All mermaids, go to the right side of the net; turtles, roll to the left on my signal. Turtles, make sure you don't get caught underneath the net, as it will roll off much faster than it rolled on! Mind your flippers!"

Sabrina watched to make sure all the mermaids had moved out of the way. Then she called to the turtles, "Roll to the left, now!"

Kimmi watched as all four turtles leaned to the left in unison, and the net rolled off their backs and into the left side of the cave. Snappy peeked out to see what was happening.

"Wow," he exclaimed. "It's great how everyone is working together! What is left to do?"

"Alleana," Sabrina called out. "There are rocks near the entrance. You and Kimmi can roll them on the end to keep the net here!"

Looking back at Snappy, Kimmi replied, "We've got to put rocks on top of it, Snappy, so it doesn't get out into the water again. Hold on, I've got to help push!"

Swimming over next to Alleana, Kimmi joined her in pushing some large rocks onto the end of the net. As she pushed, the kettle started tipping to one side.

"Kimmi," Snappy shouted out. "Remember to keep the kettle straight!"

"Yes, Snappy," Kimmi answered, quickly straightening her arms so the kettle would not tip over. "There, only one more!"

"Kimmi," Alleana said, as they got the last of the rocks pushed onto the net. "Why don't you take Snappy and head back to the caves. It has been another exciting day for you both!"

"Yes, Alleana, I would like to be back in the caves!" Kimmi said, glad she could get back to the safety of her cave. She had more than enough excitement for one day. Making sure one more time Snappy was still safe in the kettle, she headed back.

Chapter Eighteen

HOME AGAIN

As Kimmi reached her sleeping cave, she could finally relax again. She had protected her young charge, Snappy. That was her main job!

"Snappy," she called out to him with relief as they entered the cave. "You can come out now, we are back home!" She swam over to Snappy's bed and put the kettle down in front, so he could swim out and go into his sleeping place.

Slowing peeking out of the kettle at first, then sticking his head out, Snappy replied, "Thanks for protecting me and getting me home safe, Kimmi. What did you call it, a ghost net?"

"Yes, that's right. I hadn't seen one before, Snappy," Kimmi responded. "Alleana gives me lessons every day, and when I saw it, I remembered what she said about it. They are very dangerous, and we have to make sure we do not get caught in them. Then she made me memorize the steps to follow if I see one. Those lessons were very helpful today!"

Swimming over to Snappy, she continued in a concerned tone, "I'm glad we didn't get caught in it. And I'm also glad we were able to free the trapped sea creatures and make sure the ghost net could not trap anyone else. However, I was afraid you might get caught as I watched it raking the sea floor on its way toward us. It is my job to keep you safe!"

"And you did, Kimmi!" Snappy replied, reassuring her. "You remembered what you needed to do, you never left me, and you called for help!"

"But I'm now realizing you could have been hurt ... or worse! It is dangerous out there and we will have to be more careful from now on, okay?" Kimmi said softly. "I must keep my promise to your parents to keep you safe. That means I should listen to you when you are scared, so you'll have to remind me if I want to go on one of my explores."

"I will, Kimmi," Snappy replied. "You did the right thing today and we both made it back safe!"

"Yes, we did!" Kimmi said, smiling at Snappy. "And we can have lots of other adventures while you are here, but hopefully no more like today, don't you agree?"

"I agree!" Snappy said, smiling back at Kimmi. "My first two days here have had more than their share of excitement. Now, I think we can get some sleep and dream of fun adventures to come!"

"Good night, Snappy!" Kimmi replied. "We'll both get a good night's sleep and then start a new adventure tomorrow, but hopefully a nice quiet adventure!"

Kimmi made sure Snappy found a comfortable spot in the seaweed, and she stayed with him as he closed his eyes and fell asleep. Then she swam slowly over to her soft sand bed to lay down. She was physically tired from all the activity of the day, yet her mind was still racing over what had happened.

Running through each of the steps, she was glad Alleana was taking the time to teach her every day, and she realized she still had a lot to learn. She hadn't believed that a ghost net existed before, thinking it was just another story Alleana told her. But it wasn't a story, it was real! She would pay more attention to Alleana's lessons from now on, so when she encountered the dangers of the water, she will be able to remember what to do.

Then she remembered her pearls—and that there were three still missing. The clasp had ended up in the bottom of the kettle with Snappy, so when they found the last three pearls and recreated the necklace, it would be complete!

What could she do to find them? Alleana told her she could not go looking for the rest of the pearls. That was final! But something inside Kimmi was telling her she needed her necklace back, with all 41 pearls. However, she would not disobey Alleana, because it could put Snappy in danger. Snappy was her first priority!

Swimming over to the shelf where she put the 38 pearls they found; she held them in her hands. Moonlight shining through the skylight gave them a sparkly look, almost glowing as they rested on her fingers. She gazed at then, transfixed by their beauty. She didn't know why, but it stirred emotions in her she couldn't describe, only that she needed to keep the necklace with her.

She didn't know how she came to have her pearl necklace, and Alleana said it was special because it came from her before time. She still wasn't sure what "before time" meant, and she figured it may take a few more years of Alleana's lessons before she understood what Alleana was trying to convey to her.

Grabbing a large scallop shell from the floor of her sleeping cave, she carefully put all the pearls and the clasp inside it, counting each one to make sure she had 38—only three more to find! Setting the shell carefully on her shelf, she went back over to lay down in her sleeping place, the exertions of the day finally catching up with her, she was indeed very tired.

As she was about to fall asleep, Alleana swam in to check on her and Snappy.

Whispering as she swam over to Kimmi, Alleana asked, "Are you okay Kimmi? Did Snappy go to sleep already?"

"Yes, Alleana," Kimmi replied sleepily. "Snappy went to sleep a little bit ago, and I was getting ready to go to sleep now. Is everything okay?"

"Yes, Kimmi," Alleana replied. "I wanted to let you know you did well today, you followed the lessons I taught you, and in doing so you were able to summon the mermaids and rid our waters of a dangerous threat to sea creatures, big and small. You should be proud of yourself for your actions today."

"Thanks, Alleana, I will pay more attention to your lessons, I promise! Now that I know the stories you tell me are real!" Kimmi said, remembering the events of the day and the ghost net they encountered earlier. She hadn't taken Alleana's stories seriously until today. She now realized there were a lot of dangers in the water, and Alleana was teaching her how to stop them from hurting her and other sea creatures. She would pay close attention from now on!

"That's good to hear, Kimmi!" Alleana said, relieved Kimmi was finally understanding why she had to have daily lessons on living in Alleana's pod.

Moving over closer to Kimmi, Alleana whispered excitedly, "I have another surprise for you!"

Chapter Nineteen

THE LAST THREE PEARLS

"What?" Kimmi replied, a little sleepy but now concerned; she was pretty sure she didn't need any more surprises today.

"While you and Snappy were sleeping yesterday evening," Alleana replied, pausing a moment and then continuing. "Natalie and I went back and found your remaining three pearls! I wanted you to know so you wouldn't worry about them."

"You what?!" Kimmi replied in disbelief. "Really?"

"Shhh, you don't want to wake Snappy!" Alleana whispered. "Maybe if you are awake enough, we can string them now, so you can have them back when you go to sleep tonight. What do you think?"

"Yes, that would be great!" Kimmi said in an excited whisper. "I am so happy you were able to find them!"

Reaching into the small pouch at her side, Alleana pulled out the three pearls, along with a spool containing thread and a long thin needle.

"Why don't you get the rest of the pearls and then we can line them all up and put your necklace back together!" Alleana asked.

Swimming over to the shelf, Kimmi grabbed the scallop shell with the other pearls. "Here they are!" she whispered.

"Great!" Alleana replied softly. "Let's go into my cave so we don't wake up Snappy." Then she quietly turned, swimming toward her cave.

Once in Alleana's cave, she motioned for Kimmi to put the pearls down on a flat shelf. "Let's line them all up and set them in the right order so we can string them, okay?"

"Yes, that sounds good!" Kimmi agreed. Placing each pearl on the shelf, she noticed there were some bigger ones and some smaller ones, so she kept the bigger ones in the center, and the smaller ones toward the two sides.

After getting them lined up, she checked twice—counting each one and making sure the sizes were in the right place. Moving some to different places, she continued rearranging them until they were exactly the way she remembered them. "Okay, Alleana. This is how they go!" she called to Alleana.

"That looks great, Kimmi!" Alleana said. "Very beautiful the way you have arranged them. I found this also and wondered if you wanted to add it to your necklace, as it matches your hair."

Holding out her hand, Alleana revealed a large, dark red ruby. It was a stunning jewel and matched Kimmi's hair exactly. "What do you think?"

Kimmi looked at Alleana and then the ruby, it was beautiful as Alleana had said. However, something inside Kimmi was telling her not to add it to the necklace. The necklace had to remain the same!

"I'm not sure Alleana," Kimmi replied hesitantly. "It might throw the balance of the necklace off, and I feel I need to put the necklace back together like it was originally. I don't know why, but my heart is telling me it must be the same."

"I understand," Alleana responded, nodding. She could see Kimmi struggling with trying to follow her instructions, but also trying to stay true to herself and the necklace. "Your necklace shall be as it was!"

Smiling at Kimmi, she picked up the needle and thread and started putting the pearls on the string just as Kimmi had arranged them. The symmetrical pattern was very graceful, going from small to large to small again. There wasn't much difference in the size of the pearls when they were all together in the shell, but Kimmi could see the difference. Kimmi arranged the pearls as she remembered them, and Alleana wanted to make sure Kimmi's necklace from the before time was as it had been before it was broken. Alleana knew there was some connection with the necklace and Kimmi's before time, she just wasn't sure what it was.

Kimmi watched Alleana closely, making sure each pearl went in the right order on the necklace. She knew it was important, she knew it had to be exactly as before. The only thing she didn't know was why! Maybe that would come with time.

Once the pearls had been strung, Alleana attached the two parts of the clasp, one to each side. When the necklace was done, Alleana held it up to Kimmi. "What do you think?"

"It's beautiful!" Kimmi whispered, amazed by Alleana's ability to recreate her necklace. I will put it on now if it's okay!"

"Of course, Kimmi!" Alleana said as she swam around behind Kimmi to put the necklace on and clasp it together. "Now you are even more beautiful!"

"Alleana, thank you!" Kimmi said with deep gratitude. Her heart felt complete with the necklace on, she knew it was something special she had to keep, and one day she would understand why.

"Okay, Kimmi," Alleana started. "I think it is time you got some sleep, it has been a very busy day! But one more thing before you go."

Kimmi was staring at her necklace, but she looked up at Alleana to see what else they needed to talk about. She put her hand on the pearls and held them gently, making sure they didn't break.

"We need to discuss the creature!" Alleana said, her face turned serious as she looked back at Kimmi.

Chapter Twenty

A New Adventure

"What about the creature?" Kimmi asked cautiously, not sure where Alleana was going with this.

"Well..." Alleana started. "Well, one thing we have not talked about yet is that there are creatures like you saw in the waters. They are not of our world, but sometimes they do put on fins and swim awkwardly around in our waters."

"So you do know about them. What are they? How can they take their fins off?" Kimmi's mind was racing now, so many questions were flooding into her mind.

"I saw several of them, the ones with the split tails you described yesterday. They were near where you lost your pearls," Alleana explained. "We have seen them periodically, and my pod—as well as Sabrina's pod—avoid them at all costs. We have been told they are dangerous, and they are the ones who created the ghost nets, along with a lot of other dangers in the water."

"The creatures created the ghost nets? But why?" Kimmi asked. She remembered how the creature she had seen was helping to get rid of it, and it freed one of the trapped turtles. Why would it have created this danger to begin with? Maybe this creature was different—maybe it didn't create the ghost nets.

"We don't know why, except for these ghost nets are used all over by the creatures to catch sea inhabitants of all kinds," Alleana said seriously. "They are caught and dragged out of the water where they are killed. You must avoid them at all costs, that is the mermaid way. I need you to understand this, Kimmi. Please stay away from them!"

"Thank you, Alleana, for letting me know of the danger of these creatures, and that they trap inhabitants of the sea to kill them. I will remember, I promise!" Kimmi replied.

"And you will remember not to go near them, right?" Alleana replied, wanting to make sure Kimmi was getting the message in no uncertain terms—stay away from the creatures!

"I promise I will not go looking for them, Alleana, and will not follow them again—even if they look like they need help!" Kimmi said emphatically.

"Thank you, Kimmi," Alleana said with a sigh of relief. "There is so much more to learn before you will understand the many dangers in the water, and these creatures are part of the dangers you need to learn about! But you have had a very busy day, and luckily you followed your lessons. I'm very proud of you, Kimmi. You really came through today! You kept Snappy with you and kept him safe. You also remembered to signal for help when you needed it. You followed our plans like you were supposed to do, and you saved a lot of lives in the process. Thank you, it means a lot to me that today you have shown how responsible you are!"

Giving Kimmi a warm hug, she continued, "Now, why don't you go to sleep, and hopefully tomorrow will be a nice and quiet day with Snappy. His first two days have been quite exciting."

"Yes, Alleana," Kimmi answered. "I am tired and could use some sleep, and a nice, quiet day would be great!" She put her hand on her necklace once again as she added gratefully. "And thank you so much for finding the final three pearls and putting my necklace back together. I really appreciate it. You know how much my necklace means to me!"

"You are welcome, now off to sleep with you!" Alleana said. "I'll see you and Snappy in the morning!"

"Good night, Alleana!" Kimmi called back as she swam back to her sleeping cave. This had been an eventful day! And now, after everything else that happened, there was a new lesson from Alleana. The creature Kimmi had seen was a danger and she needed to stay away from it!

She would have to think hard about this. She thought it was a friend, it was helping cut the ghost net apart, and rescued a turtle. Why would it do that if it was the one who created it? Why did it wave at her? She remembered feeling this creature was a friend, that it was not dangerous.

As she fell asleep, her thoughts raced back through all the interactions with the creature—how it swam so awkwardly with a broken tail, how she had seen it take off its fins, how it had stared at her through the clear rock, and finally how it helped her to rid the waters of a dangerous ghost net.

She also thought about Snappy, and how it was her responsibility to keep him safe, no matter what! It seemed keeping Snappy safe did not mix with following the creature around, and she also remembered her promise to Alleana. She would not go looking for it, and she would not follow it around—even if it looked like it needed help.

But what if they met by accident, and the creature helped her solve a problem? What if it was the only one around to help? Kimmi's mind kept going through the events of the past two days and how the creature had been part of her adventures. If she ever did see the creature again, she would stay hidden and observe it, so she could decide if this creature was helpful or dangerous! Maybe this creature was a good creature!

As she fell asleep, she was thinking of her new friend, Snappy, and she was looking forward to their next adventure together!

THE END—*until Kimmi's next adventure!*

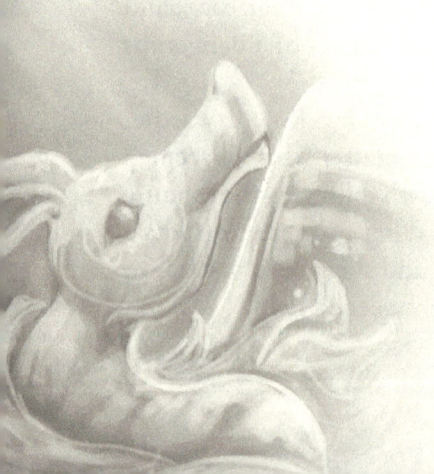

Note From The Author

Although this is a fantasy adventure, the idea of humans living underwater is a reality. It is possible for humans to create buildings under the water and reside in them for extended periods of time. Remember that water covers about 70% of the Earth's surface—what a great opportunity to live in and with the seas! I have learned of an innovative project called Nemo's Garden sponsored by the Ocean Reef Group, who are researching how to create sustainable underwater-based gardens that are not dangerous to sea inhabitants. Over the past few years, they have created numerous underwater gardens and successfully grown several crops. The Nemo's Garden group is learning how to work with the underwater ecosystem to the mutual benefit of both humans and the creatures who live in the oceans.

However, along with the good acts of some humans in today's world, there are serious threats to the ocean inhabitants that started thousands of years ago, as humans started harvesting the once bountiful oceans. Today's oceans and inland waters are threatened by overfishing, pollution, climate change, habitat destruction, and many, many other dangers.

One of these dangers is the "ghost net," and it is a real threat to the creatures of the sea! Ghost nets are abandoned, lost, or discarded fishing nets that roam freely through the oceans. And while the nets are no longer being used by humans, the nets continue to do the job they were intended to do—capture and kill sea creatures. These floating nets roam freely, trapping and killing any sea inhabitants who can't get out of their way. It has been reported that up to a million tons of fishing nets and other fishing traps end up in the oceans every year, needlessly killing fish and other ocean creatures who get trapped.

Many organizations are working to remove these deadly fishing nets from the open waters. However, until more is done to stop the abandonment or intentional disposal of nets in the oceans, this deadly menace will continue. We must all be aware of the fragile nature of the underwater ecosystems, and how easy it is to destroy them!

For more information, check out the following:
Nemo's Garden - www.nemosgarden.com and www.ocean-reefgroup.com

Worldwildlife.org - Our oceans are haunted by ghost nets: Why that's scary and what we can do | Stories | WWF (world-wildlife.org)

Earth.org - Up to a Million Tons of Ghost Fishing Nets Enter the Oceans Each Year- Study | Earth.Org

Oceanconservancy.org - : https://oceanconservancy.org/trash-free-seas/plastics-in-the-ocean/global-ghost-gear-initiative/

Book Club Questions

1. Why do the mermaids watch baby sea dragons?

2. Why did Kimmi think the creature's tail was broken?

3. How many pearls are in Kimmi's necklace?

4. How did Kimmi's necklace break?

5. What is a brain coral? What other kinds/shapes of coral are there?

6. Why does coral need to be in water shallow enough to allow sunlight to filter through?

7. How was the creature able to remove its fins?

8. Why didn't Alleana want Kimmi to look for her pearls?

9. What did Kimmi first want to do to protect Snappy once they saw the ghost net? What did she end up doing?

10. What does a mermaid sound like when she uses her siren voice?

11. How did Snappy help rescue sea creatures trapped in the ghost net?

12. What are pearls and where do they come from?

13. Are there such things as "sea dragons" in real life? What makes fantasy sea dragons different? How big do sea dragons get in real life?

14. Are there humans living underwater, for a few days and/or a few months, or even longer? Where, how, and why do they live underwater?

15. Something to think about—there are many types of human interference with the world's oceans that create a danger to large sea creatures, even if they are not being actively hunted. What effects would noise pollution, trash dumping/pollution, overfishing, heavy shipping traffic, oil drilling, and other human intrusive activities have on whales, dolphins, seals, and other mammals that live in the sea? What can be done to protect them?

About The Author

J.B. moved to Florida in her early teens and has lived there ever since, enjoying the mild weather and abundance of wildlife. She even spent several seasons raising orphan squirrels. She graduated from the University of Central Florida and has spent her working career in the legal profession. Her novels are inspired by her family and nature, as well as her need to escape from the real world once in a while.

www.facebook.com/J.B.Moonstar

Instagram@J.B.Moonstar

Twitter@jb_moonstar

Jbmoonstar.author@gmail.com

Website – www.jbmoonstar.com

Discover more by JB Moonstar

Chronicles of Ituria

Russ and The Hidden Voice

Taylor and the Red Wolf Rescue

Jenna and the Legend of the White Wolf

Jenna and the Eyes of Fire

Jan and the Secret Cave

Jan and the Search for Lilya

Taylor and the Final Nine

Michelle and the Missing Manatee

Jenna and the Broken Promise

Sara and the Secret Mission

& More Adventures to Come!

The Mermaids of Crystal Cay

Kimmi and the Sea Dragon

Roselia and the Ancient Warriors

& More Adventures to Come!

Coloring Book from

Artist Jenn Kotick

Mermaids

**Discover more at
4HorsemenPublications.com**

10% off using HORSEMEN10